THE RAINBOW ORCHID

VOLUME TWO

GAREN EWING

EGMONT

EGMONT
We bring stories to life

First published 2010 by Egmont UK Limited, 239 Kensington High Street, London W8 6SA

Copyright © Garen Ewing 2010

The author has asserted his moral rights

ISBN 978 1 4052 5047 4

1 3 5 7 9 10 8 6 4 2

Printed in Singapore

Meru – retainer to Father Pinkleton

Sir Alfred Catesby-Grey – historical researcher

Julius Chancer – historical-research assistant

Lily Lawrence – silent-film actress

Nathaniel Crumpole – movie publicity agent

Batuk – street urchin

Sepoy Sarru – soldier

Major Fraser-Tipping – of the Queen's Guides

Sujan Shah – farmer

Mr Banerji – archaeological superintendent

Mr Burke – genealogist

Newton – botanist

Urkaz Grope – businessman

Evelyn Crow – personal assistant to Urkaz Grope

Box – pugilist and henchman

General Goad – military administrator

Pendleby – assistant to Winston Attle

Winston Attle – Empire Survey Branch

Mr Drubbin – ESB field agent

Scobie – butler

William Pickle – Daily News columnist

Eloise Tayaut – aerobat

Benoît Tayaut – barnstormer

Josette Tayaut – aerobat

George Scrubbs – Daily News photographer

The Rainbow Orchid: *the story so far...*

Lord Reginald Lawrence has entered into a dangerous wager with secretive businessman Urkaz Grope over who can do best in an annual orchid competition. At stake is the Trembling Sword of Tybalt Stone and with it the Lawrence family's rights to the Stone estate, of which they have been guardians since the fifteenth century.

Meanwhile, the *Daily News* reporter William Pickle has not only published a story about Grope's secret weapon, the black pearl orchid, but he has also claimed the historical researcher Sir Alfred Catesby-Grey will enter an even rarer flower, the mysterious rainbow orchid.

Lord Lawrence decides his only chance of beating Grope's black pearl orchid is to buy Sir Alfred's flower, but he is devastated to learn that the rainbow orchid is a myth, a forgotten Vedic legend referred to only in obscure ancient texts.

However, Sir Alfred's assistant, the adventurous Julius Chancer, clings to the hope that an elderly missionary named Father Pinkleton, who claims to have actually seen the rainbow orchid, can lead them to the flower.

Against Sir Alfred's better judgement, Julius leads an expedition to India in an attempt to find the rainbow orchid and save the Stone estate from falling into Grope's hands...

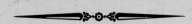

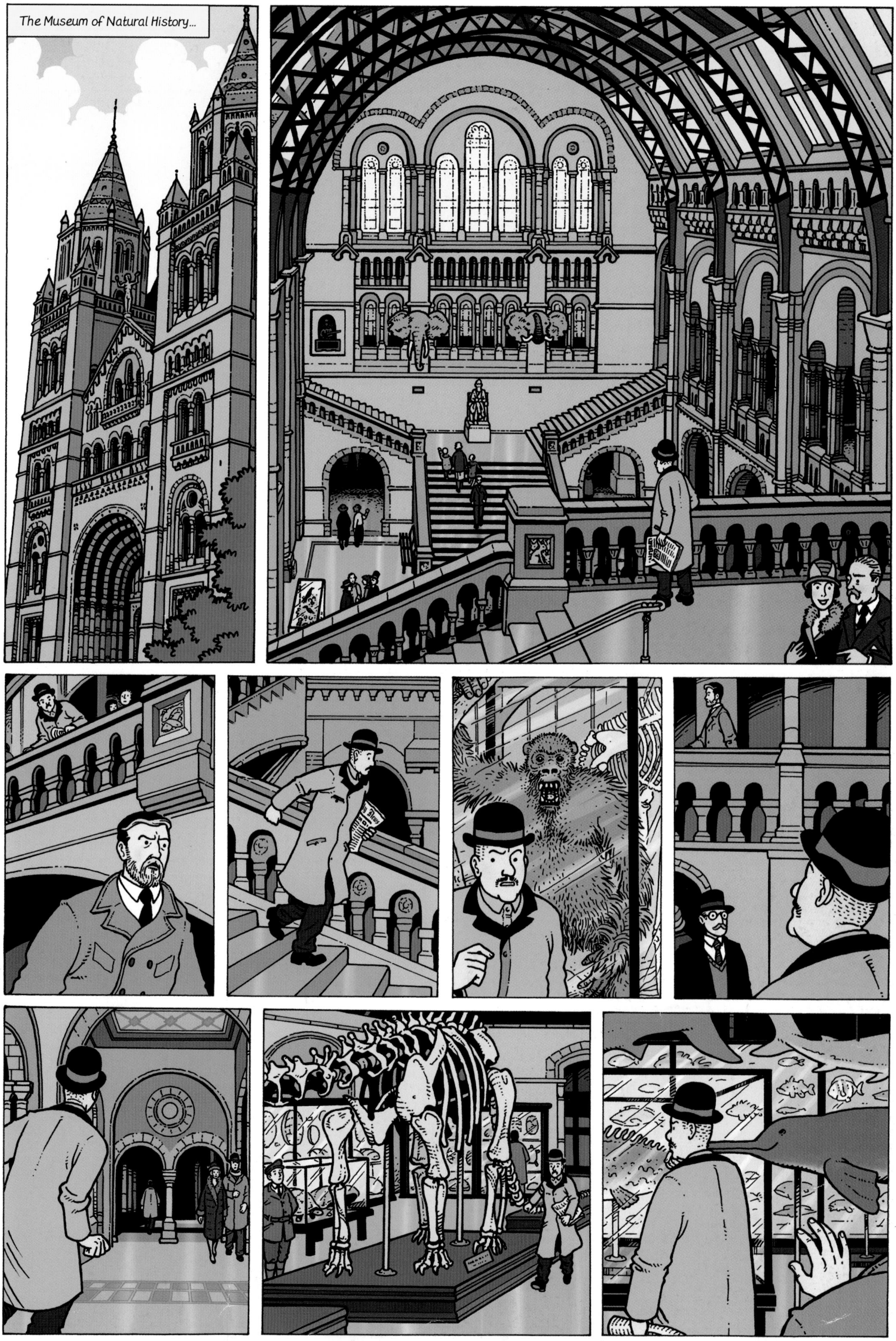
The Museum of Natural History...

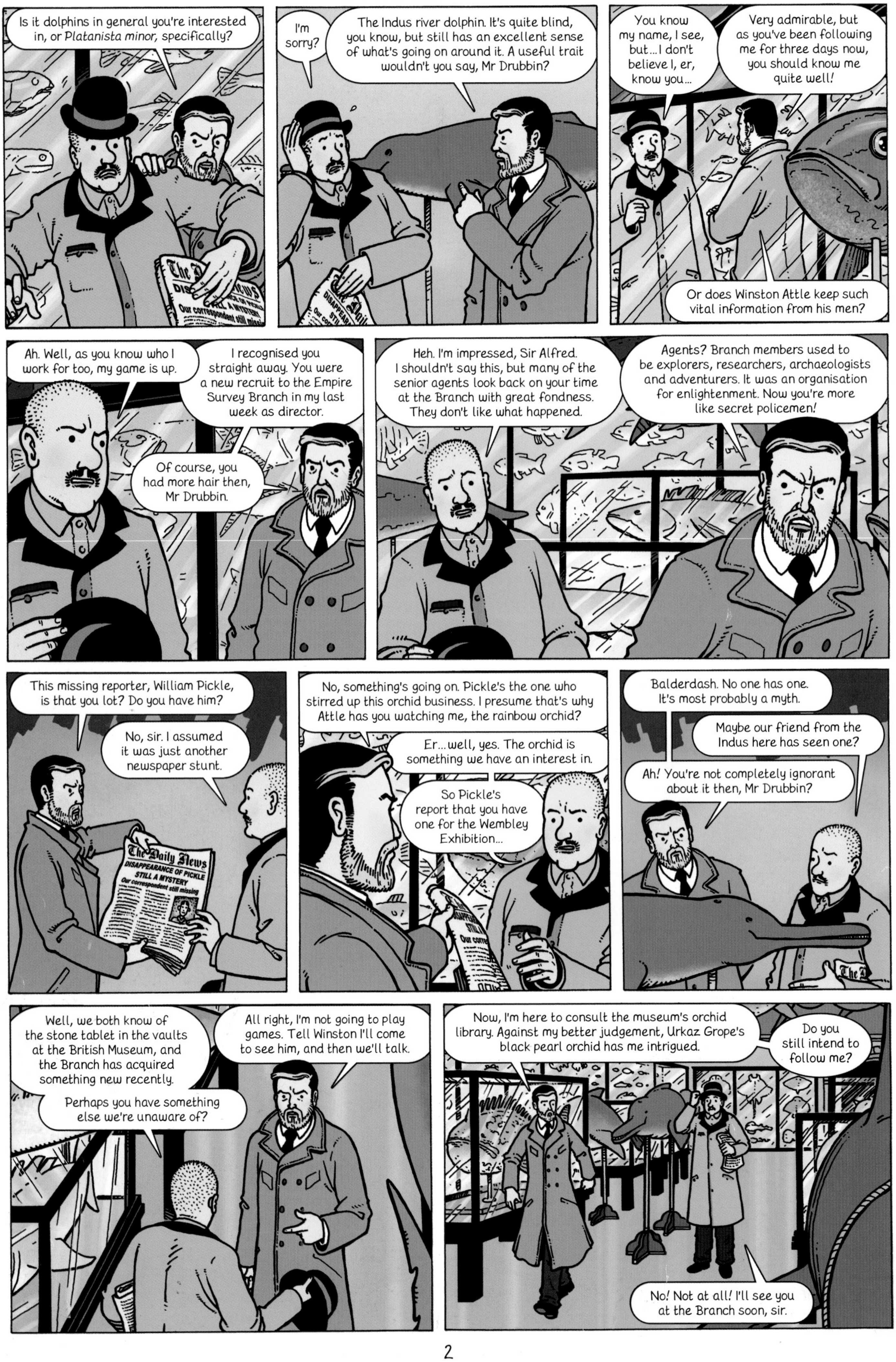
Is it dolphins in general you're interested in, or *Platanista minor*, specifically?
I'm sorry?
The Indus river dolphin. It's quite blind, you know, but still has an excellent sense of what's going on around it. A useful trait wouldn't you say, Mr Drubbin?
You know my name, I see, but... I don't believe I, er, know you...
Very admirable, but as you've been following me for three days now, you should know me quite well!
Or does Winston Attle keep such vital information from his men?
Ah. Well, as you know who I work for too, my game is up.
I recognised you straight away. You were a new recruit to the Empire Survey Branch in my last week as director.
Of course, you had more hair then, Mr Drubbin.
Heh. I'm impressed, Sir Alfred. I shouldn't say this, but many of the senior agents look back on your time at the Branch with great fondness. They don't like what happened.
Agents? Branch members used to be explorers, researchers, archaeologists and adventurers. It was an organisation for enlightenment. Now you're more like secret policemen!
This missing reporter, William Pickle, is that you lot? Do you have him?
No, sir. I assumed it was just another newspaper stunt.
The Daily News
DISAPPEARANCE OF PICKLE STILL A MYSTERY
Our correspondent still missing
No, something's going on. Pickle's the one who stirred up this orchid business. I presume that's why Attle has you watching me, the rainbow orchid?
Er... well, yes. The orchid is something we have an interest in.
So Pickle's report that you have one for the Wembley Exhibition...
Balderdash. No one has one. It's most probably a myth.
Maybe our friend from the Indus here has seen one?
Ah! You're not completely ignorant about it then, Mr Drubbin?
Well, we both know of the stone tablet in the vaults at the British Museum, and the Branch has acquired something new recently.
Perhaps you have something else we're unaware of?
All right, I'm not going to play games. Tell Winston I'll come to see him, and then we'll talk.
Now, I'm here to consult the museum's orchid library. Against my better judgement, Urkaz Grope's black pearl orchid has me intrigued.
Do you still intend to follow me?
No! Not at all! I'll see you at the Branch soon, sir.

Meanwhile, somewhere over the Arabian Sea...

That's the Baluchistan coast down there. Karachi isn't far now.

It seems so long since we stopped following the line of the caravan trail to Al Qatif.

Almost nine hours, I think. The winds in the Persian Gulf were stronger than I expected. We'll drop a little lower.

Oh, come on, Nathaniel! Did you *really* think you could get a camel on board the plane?

Yes! Well, I... I didn't realise they were that big.

But didn't you work on *The Ten Commandments?* That had camels!

DeMille expelled me from the set after one of the Rameses statues, which incidentally, I was nowhere near, toppled over on to Julia Faye and bent her feathered headdress. Anyway, I'll just have to go back to Amman and collect my camel. I paid good money for it!

Not to mention The Moabite Stone you bought. That was too heavy to bring as well, and anyway, Julius said it was a fake. The original is in Paris.

Yes, well he would tell me after I'd given that boy half my money!

CROONK!

What on earth was that?!

3

What was it? Good question! Let's see. Speed, one-twenty. Fine. Altitude, twelve thousand... eleven thousand... ten thousand... Ah.

We're dropping quite fast, aren't we? Now, what goes *croonk*? Wheel brace? No, that's *pang*! Tail flap? Hmm, more of a *krag*! Exhaust valve? A *phoom*! really. No, wait...

Petrol-pipe fracture, that's it! The engine will slacken, splutter and stop. Listen...there it goes... and there...yes! Gone! Spot on!

Can you start it again? What happens now?

Go and sit down, secure anything loose! Fasten the straps! Not you, Julius. I need you here at the controls.

Hojee!

But what can we do? We're dropping out of the sky like a sandbag! *Look!* Seven thousand feet!

TAYAUT

Why did we decide to fly? A mad idea! I shouldn't be up here! I should be on the ground, making movies! I haven't lived!

Stay calm, Nathaniel. Benoît will get us through this. Now, put your camel saddle away!

Karachi ahead! Keep the yoke steady, nose level, extend flaps. We'll try to bleed off some speed.

Cramp in my arms! Surely we can't get this on the ground, Monsieur Tayaut! We're going to crash!

There are many different kinds of crash, Julius! Steady, four thousand feet. We can level her, cross winds are favourable. Besides, the fuel hasn't caught light, and that's a very good sign.

FUMF!

Oh! I didn't expect that.

Grace

Julius! That field up ahead...

TAYAUT

It's too short! We'll end up in the trees!

Keep it central, drop the nose! We're picking up speed...hold tight, here it comes...

4

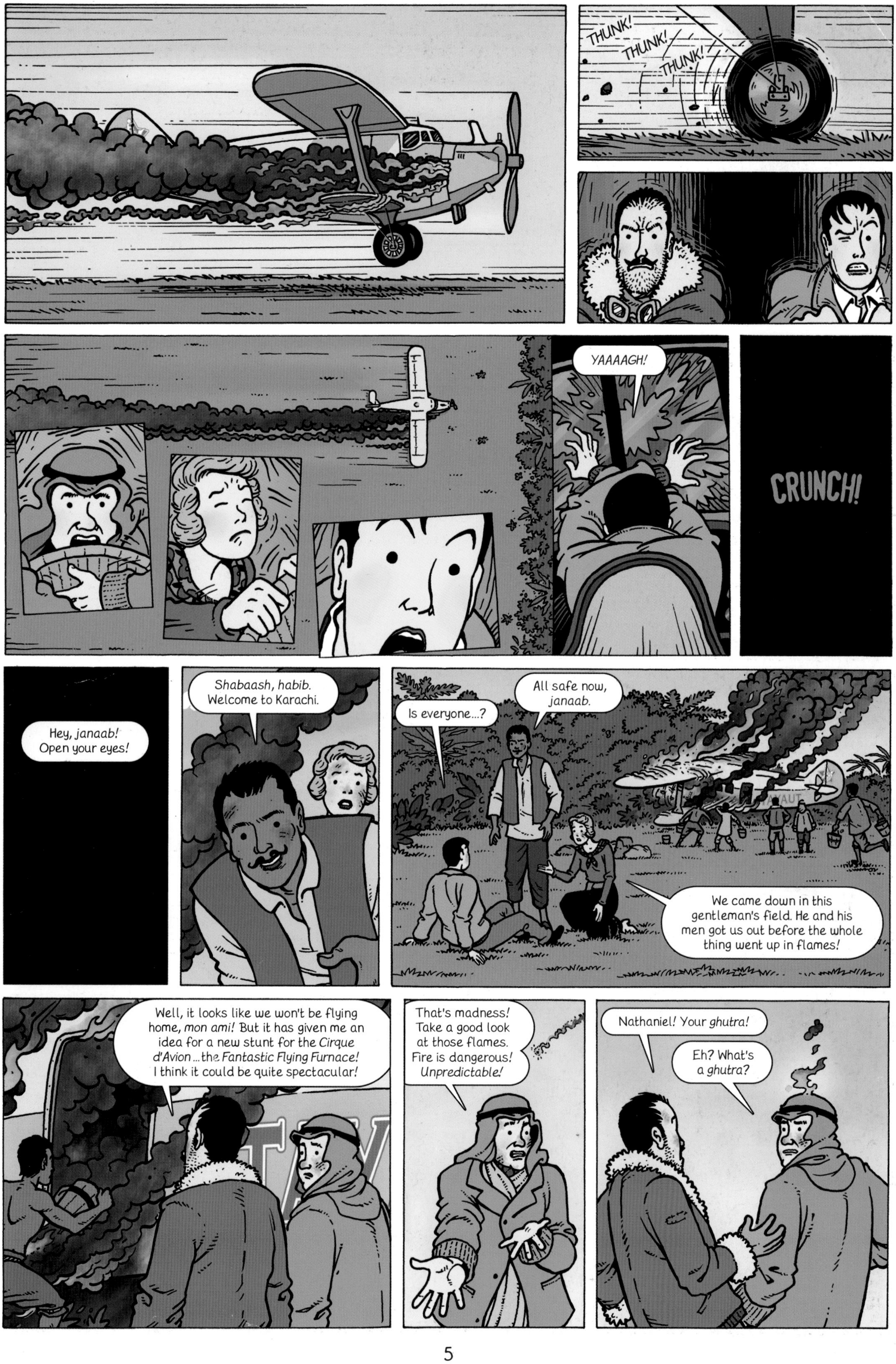

THUNK! THUNK! THUNK!
YAAAAGH!
CRUNCH!
Hey, janaab! Open your eyes!
Shabaash, habib. Welcome to Karachi.
Is everyone...?
All safe now, janaab.
We came down in this gentleman's field. He and his men got us out before the whole thing went up in flames!
Well, it looks like we won't be flying home, mon ami! But it has given me an idea for a new stunt for the Cirque d'Avion ... the Fantastic Flying Furnace! I think it could be quite spectacular!
That's madness! Take a good look at those flames. Fire is dangerous! Unpredictable!
Nathaniel! Your ghutra!
Eh? What's a ghutra?

Keep still!

Hojee! Hojeee!

PAT! PAT!

Oop! Water! Water!

WATER!

SPLASH!

Merci! Merci, beaucoup.

Hah! My camel saddle survived! Do you have camels here, sir? Of course, I own a whole camel, not just the saddle, but camels won't board planes!

Camels? Yes – oh!

WUMF!

Quick! Get the other bags away from it!

Sorry, Nat. There must have been an ember caught up in the cloth.

Fire, Nathaniel! Dangerous. Unpredictable.

Ah, my wife, Amirah.

Khush amdeed.

And I am Sujan Shah. Please, come to my house and rest yourselves.

Your entry to Karachi was not a quiet one.

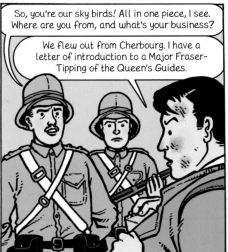

So, you're our sky birds! All in one piece, I see. Where are you from, and what's your business?

We flew out from Cherbourg. I have a letter of introduction to a Major Fraser-Tipping of the Queen's Guides.

The Guides aren't in Karachi, they're up in Peshawar. Oh... wait, there is a Fraser-Tipping at Cunningham House. I'll have to confirm all this. Right, you can freshen up, then you come with us.

Soon...

I hope there isn't too much damage to your land, Sujan.

No damage, *janaab*, we managed to stop the flames spreading. At least you are all unharmed.

You really didn't have to come with us...

I want to make sure everything is well for you. Besides, you are my guests now. If I can provide you a place to stay?

Thank you, Sujan, that is very kind.

Oh my goodness! *Look!*

GROPE GRA

KARACHI - CALC

Do you know anything about that company, Grope Grain?

No. Just one of the companies that exports wheat to the Far East, I expect.

A lot of grain goes out from the port.

Wait here, please. I'll take your letter to the Major, but if he doesn't know you, I'll have to take you into confinement until we can sort it all out.

7

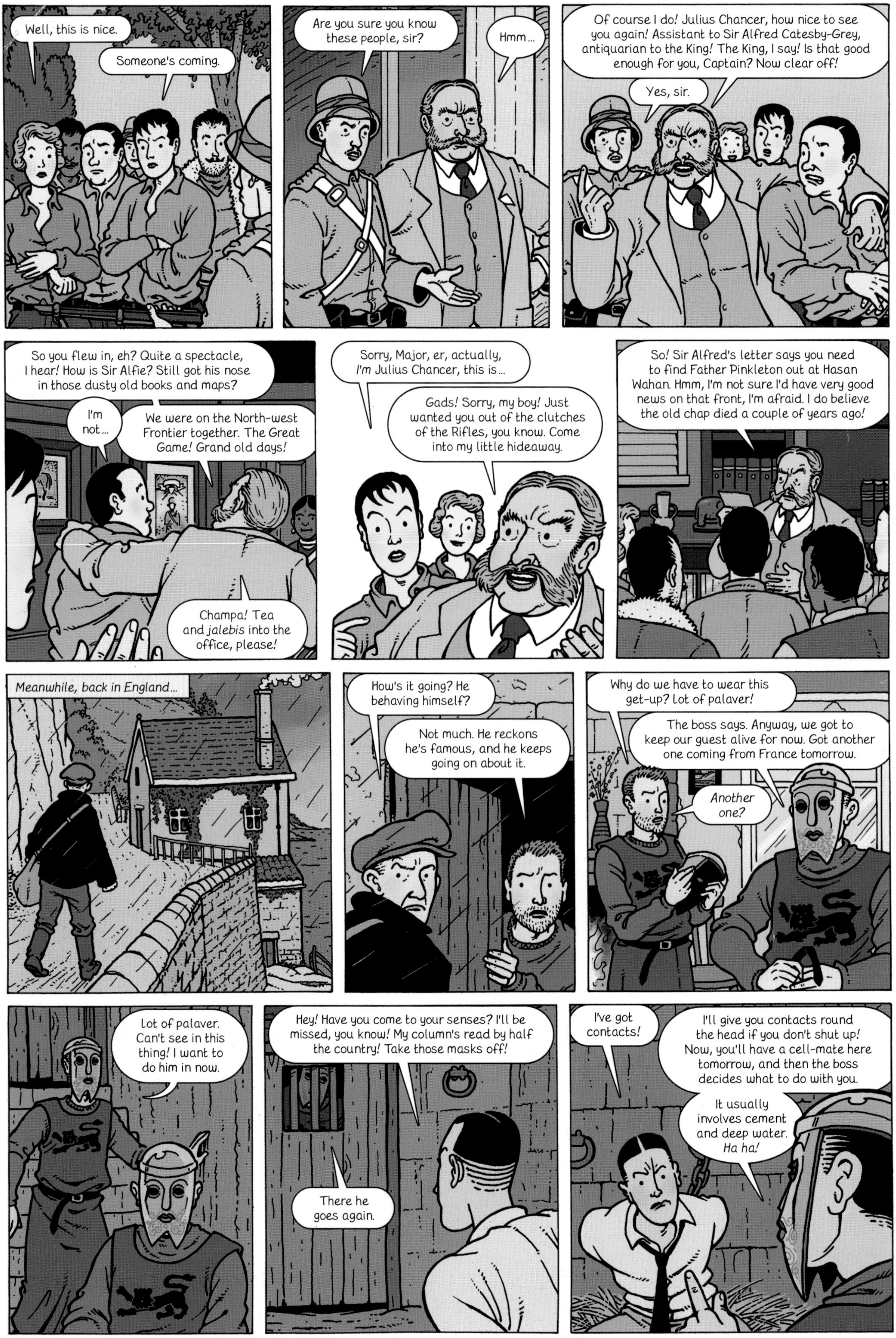
Well, this is nice.
Someone's coming.
Are you sure you know these people, sir?
Hmm...
Of course I do! Julius Chancer, how nice to see you again! Assistant to Sir Alfred Catesby-Grey, antiquarian to the King! The King, I say! Is that good enough for you, Captain? Now clear off!
Yes, sir.
So you flew in, eh? Quite a spectacle, I hear! How is Sir Alfie? Still got his nose in those dusty old books and maps?
I'm not...
We were on the North-west Frontier together. The Great Game! Grand old days!
Champa! Tea and *jalebis* into the office, please!
Sorry, Major, er, actually, *I'm* Julius Chancer, this is...
Gads! Sorry, my boy! Just wanted you out of the clutches of the Rifles, you know. Come into my little hideaway.
So! Sir Alfred's letter says you need to find Father Pinkleton out at Hasan Wahan. Hmm, I'm not sure I'd have very good news on that front, I'm afraid. I do believe the old chap died a couple of years ago!
Meanwhile, back in England...
How's it going? He behaving himself?
Not much. He reckons he's famous, and he keeps going on about it.
Why do we have to wear this get-up? Lot of palaver!
The boss says. Anyway, we got to keep our guest alive for now. Got another one coming from France tomorrow.
Another one?
Lot of palaver. Can't see in this thing! I want to do him in now.
Hey! Have you come to your senses? I'll be missed, you know! My column's read by half the country! Take those masks off!
There he goes again.
I've got contacts!
I'll give you contacts round the head if you don't shut up! Now, you'll have a cell-mate here tomorrow, and then the boss decides what to do with you.
It usually involves cement and deep water. Ha ha!

Meanwhile, in the basement of the Empire Survey Branch...

You're always after more funding, Attle. If anything, we're looking to wind down your operations further.

That would be a grave mistake, General Goad. With dark rumblings in Europe, the Branch offers a unique opportunity to stay ahead of the game.

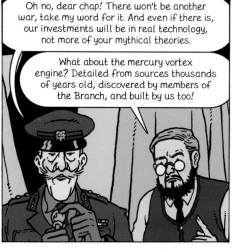

Oh no, dear chap! There won't be another war, take my word for it. And even if there is, our investments will be in real technology, not more of your mythical theories.

What about the mercury vortex engine? Detailed from sources thousands of years old, discovered by members of the Branch, and built by us too!

Yes, great fun, great fun. However, your flight experiments were a failure, Attle. It saw no use on the Western Front.

But the *theory* was sound! And there's more out there. Pendleby, the tablets.

As you know, sir, we have been accumulating material on warfare among supposed pre-ancient civilisations. Several artefacts point to some kind of decisive super weapon of enormous magnitude.

Indeed. Wonderful.

This recently discovered tablet represents one of the clearest graphic depictions we've seen.

We've translated scrolls that may suggest city-level kill power.

Marvellous. You know how to impress a military man, Pendleby. But how does this relate to the real world?

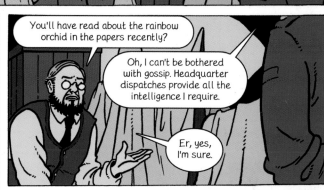

You'll have read about the rainbow orchid in the papers recently?

Oh, I can't be bothered with gossip. Headquarter dispatches provide all the intelligence I require.

Er, yes, I'm sure.

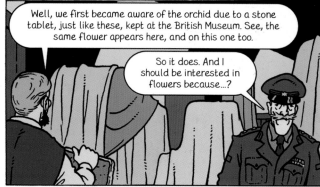

Well, we first became aware of the orchid due to a stone tablet, just like these, kept at the British Museum. See, the same flower appears here, and on this one too.

So it does. And I should be interested in flowers because...?

There's some connection, General. We believe Sir Alfred Catesby-Grey knows the whereabouts of this orchid, therefore he may have knowledge of the super weapon too.

Catesby-Grey...He was your predecessor, wasn't he, Attle? I understand he was ousted from the Branch when the War Office took over in 1916.

Something of a pacifist, if I recall.

All we need is whatever he has on the orchid. It could lead us to clues that are vital to our research.

Hm...well, if you can get Catesby-Grey on board, perhaps I can release a few thousand.

But if there's no return for us, I think that will be all the Cabinet needs to close you down for good.

9

Karachi...

CRAK!

Hmm...? Why, certainly, Mr Zukor, I'd be happy to... write... and direct... zzz...

Where do I sign?...*zzz*...

Sujan! You're up at a strange hour.

I thought I heard another engine in the sky. Did you hear it?

An aeroplane? No, I didn't!

Very unusual to hear this sound again. Sorry if I woke you, *janaab*.

Oh, I was awake already. I was just...

Well, to be honest, I was thinking how four days ago I was drinking tea with Sir Alfred in England, and now here I am, in Karachi, and, well, I'm wondering if I may have made rather a rash promise about finding this orchid!

I mean what are the chances? And I can't promise to protect Lily, or Nat, and I don't want to be responsible for... *Ha!* Sorry, Sujan! Middle-of-the-night worries!

Habib, you will find the way. It is like the moon, see? Sometimes hidden by a cloud, but always there.

Well, I suppose...oh! The moon! *look!*

Yes! There it is! I *did* hear it!

It seems to be circling.

Hmm... I don't like the look of that.

Good morning, Mister Chancer! Much nicer to see you arrive without an armed escort today!

A pleasure to see you again, Major Fraser-Tipping. Have you any news for us on Father Pinkleton?

Yes, yes indeed. But something far more exciting than that, my friends. Something I just discovered in the files. Come in! Tea's on!

An officer I know – excellent chap, wounded twice at Saran Sar – found Pinkleton's retainer, name of Meru, still up at Hasan Wahan. He confirms the old man died a couple of years ago. Locals believe he was a hundred and twenty! Ha ha!

That's the end of that line of enquiry then.

But that's all we had! What do we do now?

Well, last night I remembered I have this. Show me that tablet again.

Yes! Remarkable. The writing's the same.

Goodness! Where's the photo from?

That's the thing. A dig up at Mohenjo-daro, right next to Hasan Wahan.

I'll find out who the head honcho is up there, put you in touch.

Thank you, Major. One more thing...have you had any reports of another aircraft in the area?

In Karachi? No, I'm sure I'd hear of it. Why?

Oh, I must have been dreaming last night. Quite an experience yesterday!

Ha! You wouldn't get me up in one of those things! Just give me a pair of regulation boots, and point me to the Khyber Pass!

Why didn't you tell him the truth, Julius? That other aircraft worries me.

Let's not complicate things. We'll meet Sujan and see if he's been able to find anything out.

11

Wait a minute... Where's Nathaniel?

Ah. I think I see him...there!

Hey-ho! Guys! Look at me!

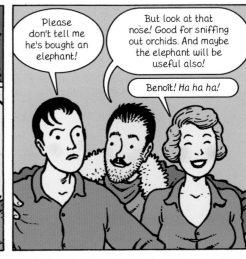

Please don't tell me he's bought an elephant!

But look at that nose! Good for sniffing out orchids. And maybe the elephant will be useful also!

Benoît! Ha ha ha!

Hssssssssssss!

RUUUAAAAAAAAA!

YAGH!

Kala nag!

Hojee!

Oh goodness!

I'm slipping! Help!

Hah!

WOOHOO!

THWAK!

CRUNCH!

Nathaniel!

A-haa! Ha! Ha! Ooh-hee ha ha! Haaha haa! Hoo!

Ow.

Nat! Are you all right?

Argh! My back! Something's out! Ow! Ow!

Hee hee!

Hey? What?

Ready?

Very funny! Circus man, yes? Ha ha!

CRIK! CRAK!

YAGH!

Ooh! That's better! I feel fine! Wow!

Hee ha ha! Circus man! Very good!

Soon...

There's Sujan!

An old potter I know in the Saddar Bazaar has a brother who saw a plane come down near a farm out at Gulba.

We'd better have a look. I can't shake the feeling that Grope has something to do with it.

They wouldn't follow us all the way to India, would they? For the sake of an orchid?

They followed us to France. As you said, Lily, Grope really does want to win that competition.

This is the place.

It's flat enough to land, but I see no sign of a plane.

Well, let's look around.

Jules! Look at this...

Oh hell.

GROPE GRAIN

KARACHI - CALCUTTA

Hey guys! I think I found it!

13

See Benoît, they managed to land without becoming a fantastic flying furnace!

What's wrong? You're white as a ghost!

That...that's one of my planes...

Wait...who's there?

Mr Chancer. Here's a meeting I didn't expect quite so soon, but you will keep coming to find us.

Evelyn Crow!

Papa! Papa, c'est moi!

Josette! Mais non!

Box, we must change our plan. Ignore stages one to six, we're skipping straight to stage seven.

My favourite...

...elimination!

Eh...?

SWISH!

Keep still!

CRUNK!

Want to run away? Go on, I'll give you a head start!

Ow!

14

Too slow, kuri!

YAAGH!

Stop! Let's discuss this!

Crumpole! Come here.

Hojee!

Hey! Come back! You were going to make me a star, remember?

Not me!

Allez, Papa!

Gak!

NUAARGGH!

Can't you just stand and fight like a man?

Why fight? Let's calm down and...

...OOOF!!

Where to now, big shot?

Keep away!

Oh, don't be like that!

Nyaa!

YAAAAAAAGHHH!

AHK!

PHUD!

Are you all right, malika?

This is getting silly!

15

Ha haa!

Ouch!

THUK!

BANG!

Non...

PAPA!

Malika, the noise will attract attention!

Ach! It's only a pocket pistol.

BOX! Get out of the way!

BANG!

POK!

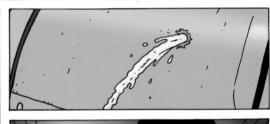

BANG!

BOOOM!

16

Somewhere on England's south coast...

Where am I? This is kidnap! When my father hears...

Quiet! Take her downstairs.

Who's speaking? Was that you?

Do you mean me?

I didn't say anything.

?

You and you! Just do it!

What are you going to do with me?

Well, if you don't behave, we'll be taking you on a nice little expedition in a rowing boat tomorrow.

Yeah. Can you swim with boulders tied round your ankles?

Hah hah! And if you do behave, we'll be taking you on a nice little expedition in a rowing boat in a couple of weeks instead.

Haaa ha haa!

I am from France. I have never heard of you.

Oh. Well, I'll have a thunderclap of a story out of this. When I get back to the typewriter, Grope won't know what's hit him.

You'll get a mention! What's your name?

Haa haa!

Who are you?

William Pickle, leading correspondent for the Daily News. Surprised, eh? Everyone must be looking for me!

Eloise Tayaut. It was Grope's banana men who snatched me on my way into town, after we chased them off the airfield.

And now I'm in England where no one will think of looking for me! So, Mr Pickle, we are going to have to escape by ourselves.

Escape?

17

Milton Square, the offices of the Empire Survey Branch...

Good to see you, Sir Alfred!

Thank you for coming.

I almost changed my mind, Mr Drubbin, but I wanted to see the old place again.

Ah! Hello, Helga, relieved to see you're still here.

She hasn't moved since Professor Buckhurst installed her in 1803.

April 1802. Discovered in a Cornish tin mine. It remains unconnected to any known mythology.

A wonderful piece.

Mr Attle will join us in the map room. This way, Sir Alfred.

I do know the map room, Drubbin. I spent four months cataloguing it twenty years ago.

Turn right down the pharaoh's corridor, then...What in the name of...?

Does chronology mean *nothing* any more?

Um...

Sesostris the Third, twelfth dynasty, followed by Mentuhotep! Eleventh!

Then Nepherites? Twenty-ninth! This is a mess.

Djoser, third dynasty. And that's not even his *serekh!* It's Teti's!

And Teti has Khufu's. Where *is* Khufu?

Oh, er...

Professor Bech will be turning in her grave!

18

Lack of attention to detail, Drubbin, is the sign of an amateur. We used to have pride in our knowledge. I won't wait long for Attle.

You've got the right stone there, haven't you, Pendleby? We don't want Sir Alfred to get a whiff of anything military!

Don't worry, sir, he'll think our only interest is the orchid.

He's here.

I hope you've used your charm to soften him up a bit, Mr Drubbin!

Er, actually...

Right. Here we go then.

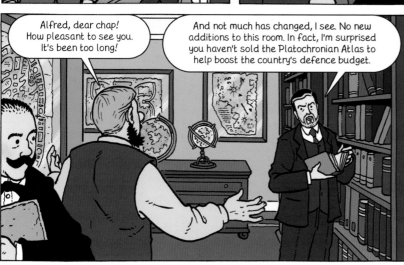

Alfred, dear chap! How pleasant to see you. It's been too long!

And not much has changed, I see. No new additions to this room. In fact, I'm surprised you haven't sold the Platochronian Atlas to help boost the country's defence budget.

Alfred, please. The war was a long time ago. Our ties with the War Office are now purely financial, and our good work continues.

There were three seventeenth-century volumes of the *Andes Cavern System* here. I worked for years to save them being lost to a Bolivian death cult. Where are they?

You see, this is why we need your help. This is why we're interested in the rainbow orchid.

Because you've lost irreplaceable and priceless books?

The Andes set is in storage, and sadly, bit by bit, more and more is being locked away in government crates. The Solomon Temple collection has gone. One of your favourites, wasn't it? You see, Alfred, they're winding us down.

What? They can't! The Branch goes back two-hundred years!

Times have changed. The age of the great exploration societies we sprang from is long forgotten. We keep ourselves busy going over old ground, Alfred. We no longer have a role in a dead empire.

And it's all about money, of course!

Not entirely. You see, I told them about the rainbow orchid. Despite your differences, the Cabinet still associates your name with a period of success at the Branch.

Imagine what it would do for us if we could bring back the orchid and show it at the Wembley Exhibition. It could lead to further expeditions.

They're interested, Alfred. They're offering us a chance!

Drubbin here says you've acquired something new connected with the rainbow orchid. What is it?

19

This tablet was unearthed last year at Jampur. You'll recall, sir, the tablet currently in the vaults of the British Museum, showing a similar flower, was found not far from there.

Yes, I have a copy of it.

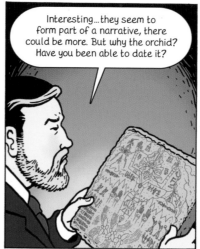

Interesting...they seem to form part of a narrative, there could be more. But why the orchid? Have you been able to date it?

The ideograms resemble those discovered at Mohenjo-daro. It could be as old as 2000 BC.

Mr Drubbin says you believe the flower is a myth, yet your assistant has gone to India to find it.

Alfred, do you have something else that supports the existence of the rainbow orchid?

All right. I have in my possession the notebook of Theophrastus.

The notebook? It exists?

And in it, while detailing several specimens sent to him by Alexander the Great from northern India, he names an orchid... *Iriode Orchino*...the rainbow orchid.

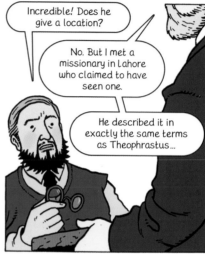

Incredible! Does he give a location?

No. But I met a missionary in Lahore who claimed to have seen one.

He described it in exactly the same terms as Theophrastus...

Dancing with light...just as it appears to be on this tablet!

What do you know about Urkaz Grope?

The black-orchid fellow? Not much but, as you know, the Branch monitors the sale of antiquities, and Grope is new on the market, spending a fortune. Mr Drubbin's been looking into it.

There's no pattern. Fifteenth-century stuff mostly, but random, uneducated buying.

He's after an antique sword that belongs to the Lawrence family. Can you look into that, Mr Drubbin?

Um, yes...well, er, I suppose so...I mean...

I can do that, Alfred. I want Mr Drubbin to accompany you to India. If you'll let us help you...if we can find a live rainbow orchid specimen, we...you, Alfred, can save the Branch!

Why should I trust you, Winston? You've lied to me before, I haven't forgotten.

Yesterday we had a report from our man in Karachi. An aircraft crashed on the outskirts of the city and went up in a fireball. One of the passengers was the film actress, Lily Lawrence.

Lawrence? Then Julius...

Your assistant is fine. All on board survived. Last we heard, they're perfectly safe.

But is he up to it? He's young, inexperienced. Let's get out there, Alfred. We have the resources, but to find the rainbow orchid...we need you!

Karachi, one mile west of the city...
Can't you gee this thing up a bit, Sepoy Sarru?
Sorry, Major, I'm afraid we'll fall to pieces if this road gets any rougher!
Never mind, it's up ahead!
Oh my goodness!
Are you the senior officer, Subedar?
No, sir. Captain Harvey, just up there.
Ah! Military Police? A party of the 14th Punjab on manoeuvres at Yowa Abad were first on the scene. What a mess!
No, no, I'm not the police! I'm looking for Chancer!
Oh, the casualties? They were all taken to the Civil Hospital, about an hour ago, I'd say. Two dead, I think it was.
What?!
They'll have some explaining to do to the MPs!
Sepoy Sarru! The Civil Hospital! At the double!
Those soldiers are going to be here all day...
Malika, what am I to do? My farm... they'll ask questions!
Do stop gibbering. Mr Grope will set you up again. Just like last time.
And you can stop looking at me as if I just stole all your comics. You're alive, aren't you?
Only just. You could have warned me you were going to blow us all to Timbuktu!
Ha! A happy accident!
Tut! Have I got soot on my nose?
What about Rajpal? Did he make it out? I didn't see him.
Oh, I expect he's hiding up a tree somewhere. We'd better get away from this place. Hopefully, we've done enough to stop Lawrence and her chums going any further.
If not, there'll be no dilly-dallying next time!

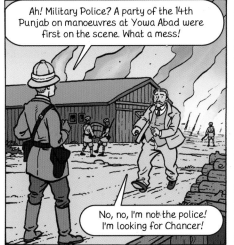

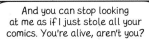

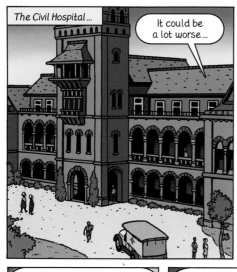

The Civil Hospital...

It could be a lot worse...

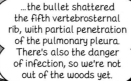

...the bullet shattered the fifth vertebrosternal rib, with partial penetration of the pulmonary pleura. There's also the danger of infection, so we're not out of the woods yet.

As for your other friend, he was dead on arrival. I'm sorry.

Huh! No friend of ours! Man-handling Lily, strangling Sujan!

Your courageous leap on to him saved my life, saheb! I am in your debt.

Oh, well, er... It's what Douglas Fairbanks would have done!

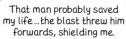

That man probably saved my life...the blast threw him forwards, shielding me.

We're all very lucky. We certainly didn't expect to see you there, Josette!

Grope's banana men returned to the airfield with that woman, Evelyn. They said they had taken my sister.

She said if I didn't fly them to Karachi, we would never see Eloise again!

I had no choice.

I flew the F2, certain we wouldn't make it. We had to make four stops for fuel, and the big man, Box, was constantly sick out the window!

We landed as soon as we saw the coast, then flew on to that farm...

And now we're here and my father has been shot...and...and I don't know where Eloise is...and how we're going to get home and find her...wuuuh!

Oh, you poor girl, it's all right, you're with us now.

This is awful. What a situation!

Thank heavens! Thank heavens! I feared the worst! All present and correct?

Don't you worry one jot, my dear! I'll send for Surgeon-Major Hatch at Jamsetjee! He saved the lives of ten Gurkhas at Ahnai Tangi!

Julius! I thought I'd be putting all your names on the casualty roll! What would I have said to Sir Alfred?

Major, that farm had a connection with Grope Grain. It was Urkaz Grope who...

Yes, I saw. Investigations are underway. If they're still in Karachi, they won't get far.

Now, I can't have those clod-hopping rhinos in Military Police interrogate you, Miss Lawrence! I'll take all your statements myself tomorrow.

What you need to do is get clean and get some rest. Then you can look to getting on with this orchid business.

I'm not sure that's a good idea any more. Eloise kidnapped, Father Pinkleton dead, Monsieur Tayaut almost killed! I don't know if it's worth it...

Julius, what are you saying? We can't give up! My father...

Friends, perhaps now is not the best time to make a decision.

Please, back to my farm! It is safe and quiet, and Amirah makes a most exquisite haleem!

Excellent idea! I'll get Sarru to drive you. Things will look different after a good night's sleep.

That night...

I've got the orchid, Julius.

No. It's here. This is it.

I have the real orchid. Take it!

That's the end, Jules. Come home.

Sir Alfred?

You are having a dream. Back to sleep.

Next morning...

KAA-KA-ROO!

Julius, we can't return to England without even trying. My father stands to lose everything!

Let's just get to the hospital. We'll discuss things later.

What about all the money we've spent? We're relying on you! Are you listening?

Sorry, Lily, I didn't sleep well last night. I thought there was... Do you think we're being followed?

Stop trying to change the subject! This is important!

You know, when one of my scripts is turned down, or I'm told yet again I'm not ready to direct a picture, I say to myself, Nat...

...Nat, I say, don't let them beat you down! You prove them wrong! When things get grummy, that's when you have to hit all the sixes!

Let's speed up a little. I'm certain we're being followed.

Well, I can't see anything!

23

After he woke up and started pointing out all his other scars to the nurses, we decided to move him outside for some fresh air.

Sounds like he's coming back to life!

I'm fine, I'm fine. Just don't make me laugh. Or breathe!

Don't listen to him, he's been breathing all morning!

And we'll have you laughing in no time! Wait until you hear my latest bag of bone-ticklers...the one about the vicar and the three flappers...er, or was it three vicars?

Ha ha! Ow! Don't start, Nathaniel!

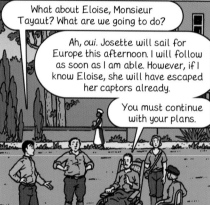

What about Eloise, Monsieur Tayaut? What are we going to do?

Ah, oui. Josette will sail for Europe this afternoon. I will follow as soon as I am able. However, if I know Eloise, she will have escaped her captors already.

You must continue with your plans.

What plans? Julius doesn't think it's worth it any more!

What? Pourquoi?

Your daughter has been kidnapped. We've completely destroyed two of your aircraft. You've been shot – almost killed, all thanks to this mythical orchid!

On top of that, Father Pinkleton, our only solid lead, has been dead for two years.

If Eloise has been kidnapped for *nothing*...if my planes are lost for *nothing*...if I've been shot for *nothing*... For this bullet hole – you *must* find the orchid, Julius!

But surely...

No. No, you're right.

It will not be for nothing, Benoît. Now we must do *everything* we can to find the rainbow orchid.

I'm sorry, Lily.

It is true we wouldn't be in this situation if it wasn't for your quest! But we are each responsible for our own choices and actions!

Chacun son chemin! Chacun son destin!

Ha ha! She gets that from her mother.

True spirit!

If nothing else, I want to show Evelyn Crow and her boss they're not going to stop us that easily! There must still be things we can do.

The village where Pinkleton worked as a missionary, where he actually saw the orchid...

We're going to need Major Fraser-Tipping to supply us with new equipment...

And here comes the old man! Who's the tall chap with him?

Sound the *reveille*! Everyone up and about, that's what I like to see!

Friends, this is Meru. He came to see me last night, and...well, I'll let him explain!

I was attendant to Father Michael Pinkleton. The Major's enquiries in the name of Sir Alfred Catesby-Grey bring me here.

Have I seen you somewhere before? You were following us this morning, weren't you?

I came in search of Catesby-Grey. The Major tells me you are his representative. There is something you need to see.

Is it to do with the rainbow orchid?

It is to do with Father Pinkleton's will. I believe it will be of great interest to you, but you must come to Hasan Wahan to see.

How can we be sure this isn't a trap and you work for Urkaz Grope?

I can vouch for him, Julius. It was Meru we contacted regarding Father Pinkleton.

I was his faithful retainer for ten years. For the past two years, I have been keeper of his affairs and estate.

Don't forget the writing on your stone tablet. Pinkleton lived right on top of Mohenjo-daro!

And if he had papers or maps...

It seems the trail's not such a dead-end after all. Hasan Wahan it is, then!

Meanwhile...

Here he comes!

I wouldn't say you blend in exactly, but it's an improvement on the smouldering rags.

And I can get a new hat made in the bazaar!

Malika! I'm back! I found out Rajpal was taken to the Civil Hospital. He...he's dead!

A happy accident was it? You killed him!

You will let go of me.

Right now!

We are here to do a job for Mr Grope. If anyone wants out, they're free to go.

But remember – Mr Grope is not forgiving of those who fail him. And I do not intend to fail him!

25

England...

Mr Burke!

Good morning, Newton. How's business?

Not too bad, thanks. The orchid is doing well, so that means I'm doing well.

And your work?

Oh, well, last week, I drew up a very nice chart showing Urkaz Grope's ancestry, and his direct line back to the knight, Sir Artus Grope. Just a shame it's a complete fabrication!

What do you mean?

Remember Mr Herber, my predecessor? He conclusively proved that Urkaz Grope's ancestral line does not connect with Sir Artus. Different Grope family. The Artus line died out in 1412, you see.

The thing is, since giving Grope that news, Mr Herber seems to have died out as well. No one's seen him for five weeks.

So now I find anything Grope wants. I'm a traitor to the truth of history, but what choice do I have?

I know the feeling...

CLONG!

You're both late.

Mr Burke, at last! Is that what I hope it is?

We finally tracked it down in Brussels. I do fear you have paid far more than it is worth, sir.

Money is no object. This is invaluable to me.

Mr Grope, I was wondering... erm, what's become of Pickle, the reporter? Will you release him? You know...eventually?

Pickle? Unlikely. He'll be disposed of soon enough. You just concentrate on our orchid, that's all you should be worrying about. It looked a little dry this morning, I thought.

Ah, yes! This is incredible!

Sir Artus Grope. There's no doubt I am his heir! See the resemblance?

Yes sir. Really... amazing.

Um...I don't see it.

What? Look man! The eyes!

Newton!

Oh, er...yes. I see it now, yes.

The last of the Council of the Order of the Black Lion...before it was mistakenly passed on to those pathetic weaklings, the Lawrence family, and died out!

Don't worry, Sir Artus! Soon the Grope name will be great once more...and the Black Lion shall return!

26

Karachi Cantonment railway station...

Messages dispatched?

Yes, a telegram sent to Sir Alfred to say we're leaving Karachi.

And the same to my father.

Sepoy Sarru will accompany you as far as Hasan Wahan, and this compartment on the train is all yours.

I've bamboozled the commissariat with paperwork and liberated some kit for you, though you may need to hire some spare legs further on.

Ey!

You need a dhodi? I can help! I'm strong! My mother was born in Simikot, so I'm a Sherpa! I know all the good kulis from here to Lahore!

I am Batuk!

Juldi juldi! Train is leaving!

Ha ha! Looks like you're in good hands! Best of luck, my friends!

Goodbye, Josette. Don't forget to contact my father if you need anything at all to help find your sister.

Thank you, Lily. I'm sure all will be fine.

Bon voyage, Julius Chancer. Return with the orchid and we will stage a spectacular air show for you in Cherbourg!

Then I promise I'll be there!

27

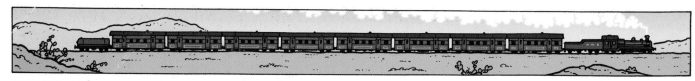

...and that's when I ran away from home to see the world! Three of my sisters live in Lahore, two in Rawalpindi and one in Peshawar, so I'm free to travel all over and stay with them when I want. And I know everyone useful! Just ask!

Are you rich, *sahiba*?

Um ...

You bet she is, kid! This is Lady Lily Lawrence, and not only that, she's a world-famous movie actress! Want her autograph?

Oh, Nathaniel! Don't call me Lady.

Movies! Charlie Chaplin! *The Kid!* Just like me! How did you make yourself a lady actress, *sahiba*?

Well, Batuk, I ran away from home when I was young too.

Did you really?

Don't look so surprised! I wanted to be a great dramatic stage actress. Ellen Terry and Sarah Bernhardt were my idols after I played Miranda in the school Shakespeare.

After my brother was killed in the Great War, I lost myself in the magical world of the theatre.

Father disapproved, and one drunken night he burnt all my biographies and postcards.

Glennie, our old chauffeur, used to drive me secretly to auditions, and when I got a part in a play, that was it, I packed and left!

The play was dreadful! Two of the actors had a fight over me, so I escaped to America and got some work in films.

Cheap comedy two-reelers at first, until I got my big break at United Players.

Lady Macbeth! Josephine! Ayesha! Joan of Arc! Lily Lawrence has played all the greats!

Like you, Lady *sahiba*, I ran away from home, and I too will become great! Although I have six sisters, I would like you to be my big sister number seven. I will call you Didi!

Thank you, Batuk, I am most honoured.

Now watch this! Here is Charlie Chaplin!

We are about to stop at an outpost on the edge of Dokri. It is unscheduled, so we must disembark quickly.

They want one rupee for each mule and three to hire the cart.

Well, that sounds reasonable.

No! I said eight anna for the cart and four for each mule.

Right. What did they say?

Then they say four rupees for everything!

Oh, well...that sounds good.

Not good, Didi. I say one rupee for cart and six anna for each mule. Final offer!

Ah. And...?

They agree.

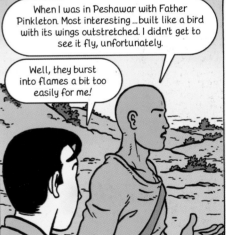

Major Fraser-Tipping told me you used flight to travel to Karachi, is that so?

Flight? Yes, well, most of the way, ha ha! Bit of a bumpy landing. Um...have you seen an aeroplane before, Meru?

When I was in Peshawar with Father Pinkleton. Most interesting...built like a bird with its wings outstretched. I didn't get to see it fly, unfortunately.

Well, they burst into flames a bit too easily for me!

Has anyone seen Batuk? I don't think I've seen him since we left the outpost!

Here I am, Didi! Making sure nothing is left behind!

I was worried. Hey, where's your neck-tie? Have you lost it?

Ey! I must have left it on the train. Oh, well!

29

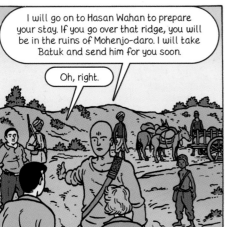

I will go on to Hasan Wahan to prepare your stay. If you go over that ridge, you will be in the ruins of Mohenjo-daro. I will take Batuk and send him for you soon.

Oh, right.

A bit odd.

Hm. Well, let's look around.

No further! No trespassers! Stay back!

Oh, sorry, I thought you were scavengers, thieves, plunderers! You're not, are you?

I'm Julius Chancer, assistant to historical researcher, Sir Alfred Catesby-Grey.

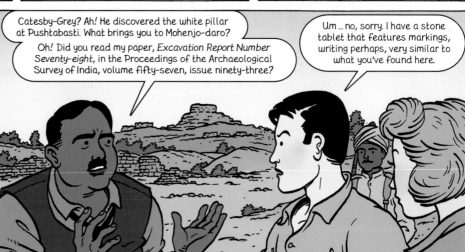

Catesby-Grey? Ah! He discovered the white pillar at Pushtabasti. What brings you to Mohenjo-daro?

Oh! Did you read my paper, *Excavation Report Number Seventy-eight*, in the Proceedings of the Archaeological Survey of India, volume fifty-seven, issue ninety-three?

Um ... no, sorry. I have a stone tablet that features markings, writing perhaps, very similar to what you've found here.

Ah, the seals. Let me show you...

Mohenjo-daro was once a great city, part of a great civilisation! They traded as far as Mesopotamia. We've uncovered streets, drains, temples, granaries. An Indian culture as great as the Ancient Egyptians'!

What happened to them?

We don't know. War? Drought? Floods? Many questions remain ... including the mystery of their indecipherable writing.

These are the seals. An elephant.

A god? An early form of Shiva?

And this ... My colleague, Mr Spencer, thinks it's a unicorn. Hah!

What about flowers? Have you seen anything resembling an orchid, perhaps?

Orchids? No, but see this figure...

She appears to have a headdress of flowers, I don't think they're orchids, but ...

HEY!

You! Trespasser! Thief! Stay back!

It's all right! That's Batuk, he's with us!

30

Mr Meru says to come now! He says to hurry!

Meru? Old Pinkleton's retainer? I'd stay away from him if I were you!

Why? Did you know Pinkleton?

I attended his funeral a couple of years ago. Very strange man. And I know for a fact that Meru has taken artefacts from my site! If I ever catch him...

Come! We must hurry!

Thank you Mr, er...?

Banerji. Don't forget to read my paper! Volume fifty-seven! Issue ninety-three!

Mr Meru says to be urgent!

What can be so important?

Dinner, I hope!

Hasan Wahan is this way, Batuk.

Meru's house is away from the village. This way!

There's not much time. Through here...

What's going on, Meru?

Sepoy Sarru, Batuk, can I ask you wait outside, please.

Ey! I want to see what it is!

What...?!

...Father Pinkleton?

Alfred? Alfred Catesby-Grey...

He thinks you are Sir Alfred. He does not have long.

We...we were told you were dead!

Heh. I am old. When I first came to India, Combermere was marching on Bharatpur.

Combermere? But...that was in 1825!

Yes...a long time ago. My longevity lead the locals to believe I was an evil spirit! Things became uneasy, then dangerous. Eventually Meru staged my burial so I could see my last days in peace.

Now, at last, my time has come.

You...you remember the orchid, Alfred? That is why you are here. Many years ago, when I was a missionary in Chitral...

I saw it!

I gave up everything and searched the mountains, the valleys, for five long years before I saw it again.

Where, Father Pinkleton? Where did you see the rainbow orchid?

31

You wish to see it? Then you must take Meru back to his people...his home! There the orchid grows.

But...

Meru!

Promise me! He must go back to his...

Yes, my Father?

Domasti yovantu ka yava tu, Meru. Otu domasti tu ka iikse pala...

Anu savra eska sama, Babata, aham asim daravnu yovantu ka ma sviikota ahama domasti.

Alfred ka kari eska. Aham zradsa saya.

You will...see your home...again...

He has passed.

Oh! Oh no...

Do you really think Pinkleton was that old?

It's possible, but it would make him over a hundred and twenty at least.

I had a look at his maps – they're far more detailed than anything I've seen at the Royal Geographical Society. If only Sir Alfred could see them!

Too bad Sir Alfred wanted to stay at home with his old books. How did you end up working for that grumpy old goat, anyway?

Wait, don't tell me! He found you as a street urchin and brought you up among the exhibits in his private museum!

Hah. You think I'm another runaway do you?

Well? Are you?

Oh, you really want to know?

Of course! Come on then – runaway or museum urchin?

32

Well, how about farm boy? I was brought up on a farm, though after my father was killed in an accident my mother and two uncles had to sell up and move off the land.

When I was fourteen, my uncles went off to the war in France. I wanted to go over and fight with them, so I lied about my age and joined up too.

Within a month I'd been shipped off to Gallipoli instead. That was a bit of shock!

One day we were given the job of extending the trenches out on the Kerves Spur. While digging I unearthed some kind of ancient statue. One of the officers had it sent back to the British Museum.

Anyway, the fun didn't last. That night the Turks went all out. As if the shells weren't bad enough, rain flooded the trenches, threatening to drown us if we stayed put!

Three of us climbed out the wrong side and soon found ourselves stranded in the middle of no-man's land. We had to hide in the scrub for two days with no water.

Then I spotted a small cave entrance — so we crawled in!

Inside was a network of tunnels, full of carved stonework just like the statue I'd found. We ended up in a huge cavern full of ruins, and also an entire Turkish division commanded by German officers.

I had no idea what they were up to, but it didn't look good. Chas threw a jam-tin bomb into a huge vat of hot oil, and we ran for our lives!

BOOM!

We made it back to the trenches, but lost Artie to a mine, and I got a bullet in the hip. We watched the flames over Achi-Baba. Whatever it was the Turks were planning, we'd stopped them.

I was shipped off to Malta to convalesce and suffered an endless stream of Intelligence officers interrogating me about the enemy's military strength.

One was different though. All he was interested in were the ruins and the statue I'd found. He was from something called the Empire Survey Branch. It was Sir Alfred.

After meeting him, I became fascinated by his work and tried to get a job at the Branch when I returned to England, but they wouldn't have me. Then Sir Alfred left to set up on his own. My persistence paid off, and he took me on as his assistant.

And now here you are, helping a film star to find a flower, sitting in the desert somewhere in India. Though, I must say, for a desert it's absolutely freezing!

Hah, sorry, I gave you the full life story!

Well, I did ask. Anyway, I'm glad I did. It's good to know you a bit better. I mean, you know, as a travelling companion...

Oh, of course, yes! Speaking of which, we'd better get back. Sepoy Sarru is heading back to Karachi tonight, and we can see if Nathaniel's kept that kettle warm!

Later that night...

You have been asked a difficult task in taking me to my homeland. It is far into the mountains.

Well, if that's where the orchid grows...

I was cast out from my people. Father Pinkleton argued my case, but they would not listen, so he left with me. He was a true friend.

Um, why did your own people cast you out? If you don't mind me asking...

Ah... let us say it was because I fell out of favour with a person of influence. But much time has passed since then.

The flower you seek does grow there. It brought Father Pinkleton to my homeland, where it has great significance.

Have you seen the rainbow orchid, Meru?

I have. They are rare, but Father Pinkleton realised his ambition to find one. If our journey is successful, I hope you will be as fortunate.

Well, it seems we have quite a trek ahead of us. Let's get some sleep, and tomorrow we'll make a plan.

England...

Scrubbs? Mr George Scrubbs of the Daily News?

Yes.

And you're Newton? Your message said you had information about William Pickle!

First, promise – this is not for publication. Pickle is in grave danger, and if this appears in the press, he'll be dead, I'll be dead, you'll be dead!

Oh. Er, all right.

Take this.

Fancy dress?

There's a footpath that leads from Chalksea to Little Trilling on the coast. Meet me the day after tomorrow at eight in the morning. Wear this outfit.

What?! Is this a practical joke?

It is very serious, Mr Scrubbs. Don't let anyone see you. I'll be dressed likewise.

This is crazy!

If you want to save Pickle then you must do it. Eight o'clock, Mr Scrubbs!

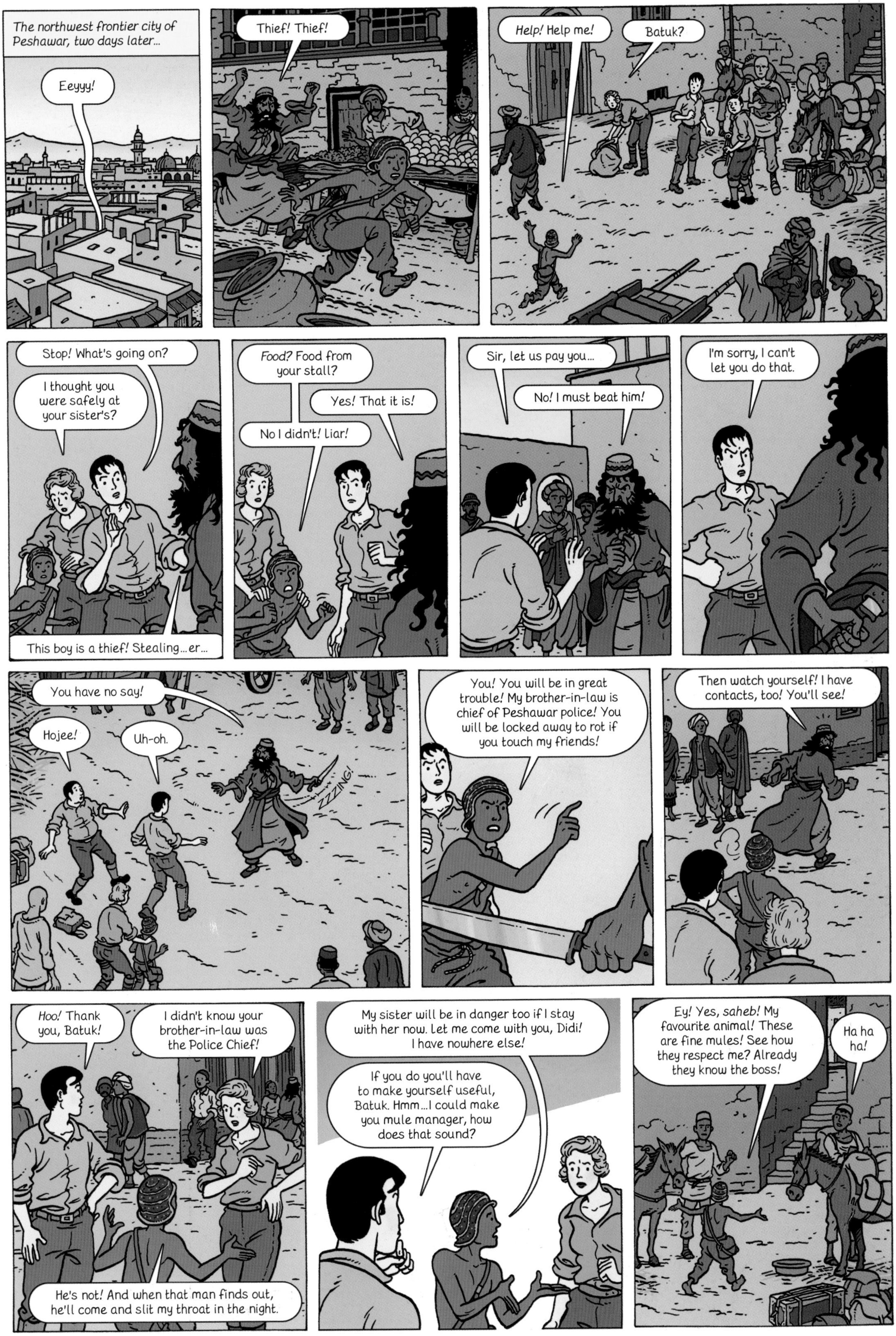

The northwest frontier city of Peshawar, two days later...
Eeyyy!
Thief! Thief!
Help! Help me!
Batuk?
Stop! What's going on?
I thought you were safely at your sister's?
This boy is a thief! Stealing... er...
Food? Food from your stall?
Yes! That it is!
No I didn't! Liar!
Sir, let us pay you...
No! I must beat him!
I'm sorry, I can't let you do that.
You have no say!
Hojee!
Uh-oh.
ZZZING!
You! You will be in great trouble! My brother-in-law is chief of Peshawar police! You will be locked away to rot if you touch my friends!
Then watch yourself! I have contacts, too! You'll see!
Hoo! Thank you, Batuk!
I didn't know your brother-in-law was the Police Chief!
He's not! And when that man finds out, he'll come and slit my throat in the night.
My sister will be in danger too if I stay with her now. Let me come with you, Didi! I have nowhere else!
If you do you'll have to make yourself useful, Batuk. Hmm... I could make you mule manager, how does that sound?
Ey! Yes, saheb! My favourite animal! These are fine mules! See how they respect me? Already they know the boss!
Ha ha ha!

The next day...

Dhal for dinner! My number two sister's recipe, very good!

Nathaniel! It's ready! Where is he?

Guys! Look who I found trying to get at the biscuits in my backpack! What a cutie!

That is cub of *barfani chita!* Very dangerous, *saheb!* You should not have!

Aw, he's harmless! I think he must be lost. But you found my biscuits didn't you? Oochi-coo! Heh!

raaow!

It is a great risk, Nathaniel. We do not want a mother snow leopard after us. Come, we will find a safe place to put him.

Aw, man! All right. Come on little kitty...

We will keep the fire going tonight and stay close.

You and your animals, Nathaniel!

Morning...

Look at that! What a climber.

It's a markhor. Want it for your collection, Nat?

Yeah, yeah. Hilarious.

We wouldn't have you any other way, Nat.

GRAAOOOWW!

Hojee!

Grraaow... grrrrr...

Nobody move!

A snow leopard! This is very unusual behaviour...they normally stay well away from people.

Nathaniel!

Is there something you'd like to tell us?

No! Like what?

roaaw!

Right! Don't worry! I'll return him to his mother — now she's decided to take responsibility. Glad to help!

GRRAAAAOOOOOWW!!

Ho...ho...j-jee!

Nat?

Nat?

Crikey. Here...

Grrrrrrrrr...

roaaw!

Easy, my friend...

37

Right. Well that's that. Let's go on.

Batuk? What are you doing?

Ey! To find our way back! We are going far, and I'm scared we will get lost!

There is no need to fear. Julius Chancer will make sure you get home safely. Why have you got all those...

My feet hurt, Mr Meru! Look!

Hm. You were not prepared for this journey. I will sew you some shoes at camp tonight.

Come. Climb up for now.

Ey!

Where's Batuk? Someone always goes missing when dinner's ready!

He went to try out the shoes I made.

I don't like him wandering around in the dark. We're so high up now.

Tell him I'll have his dinner if he's not quick! This is good!

Batuk!

Batuk? Where are you?

Bat...? Oh... no...

Ah. Greetings, Miss Lawrence!

Sorry, Didi.

38

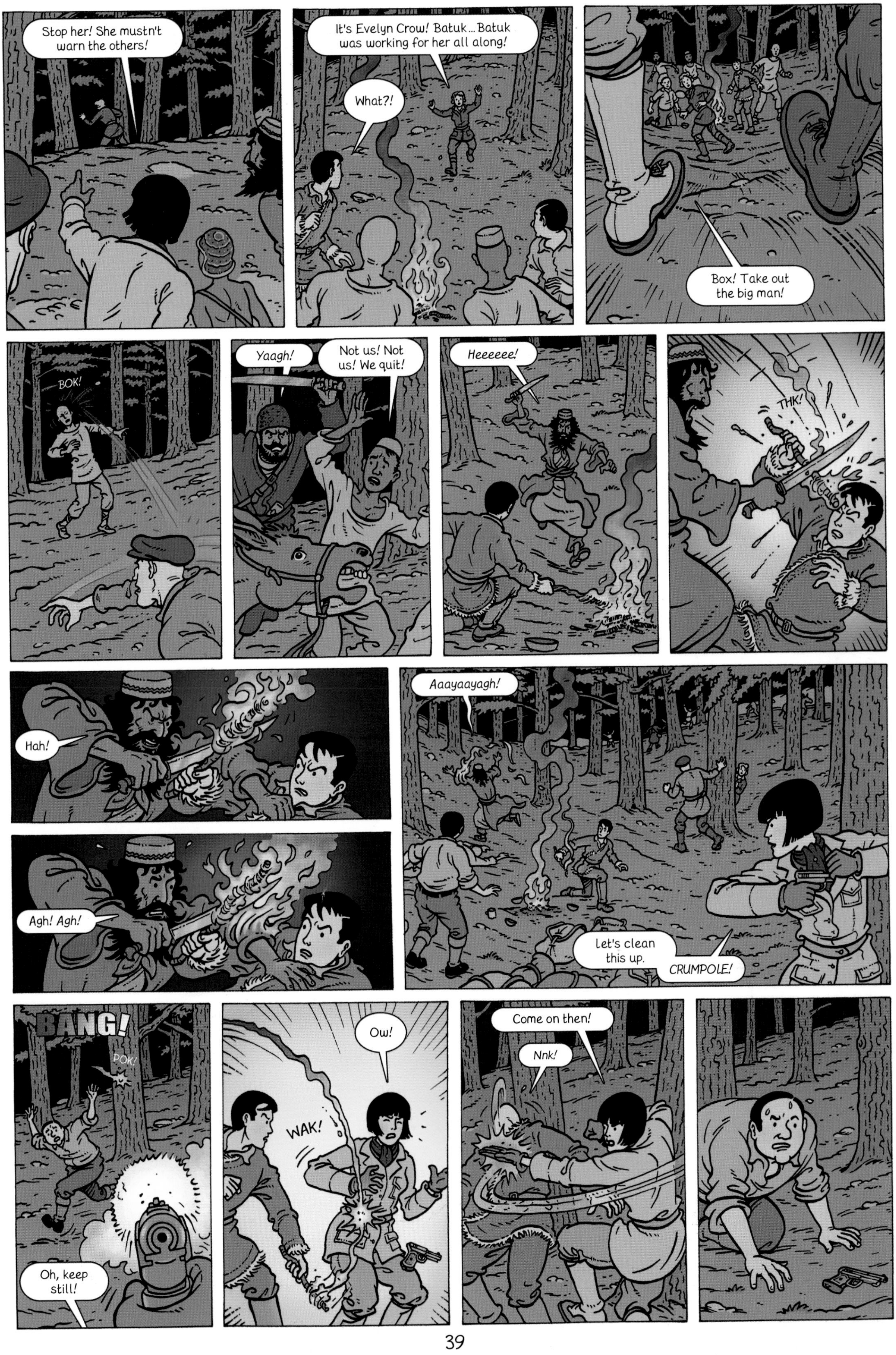
Stop her! She mustn't warn the others!
It's Evelyn Crow! Batuk... Batuk was working for her all along!
What?!
Box! Take out the big man!
BOK!
Yaagh!
Not us! Not us! We quit!
Heeeeee!
THK!
Hah!
Agh! Agh!
Aaayaayagh!
Let's clean this up.
CRUMPOLE!
BANG!
POK!
Oh, keep still!
Ow!
WAK!
Come on then!
Nnk!

Can this really be the end of the quest for the rainbow orchid? The adventure concludes in Volume Three!

THE RAINBOW ORCHID
VOLUME THREE

The adventure concludes in Volume Three as Urkaz Grope finalises
his villainous scheme and the quest for the rainbow orchid leads
Julius Chancer into uncharted territory.

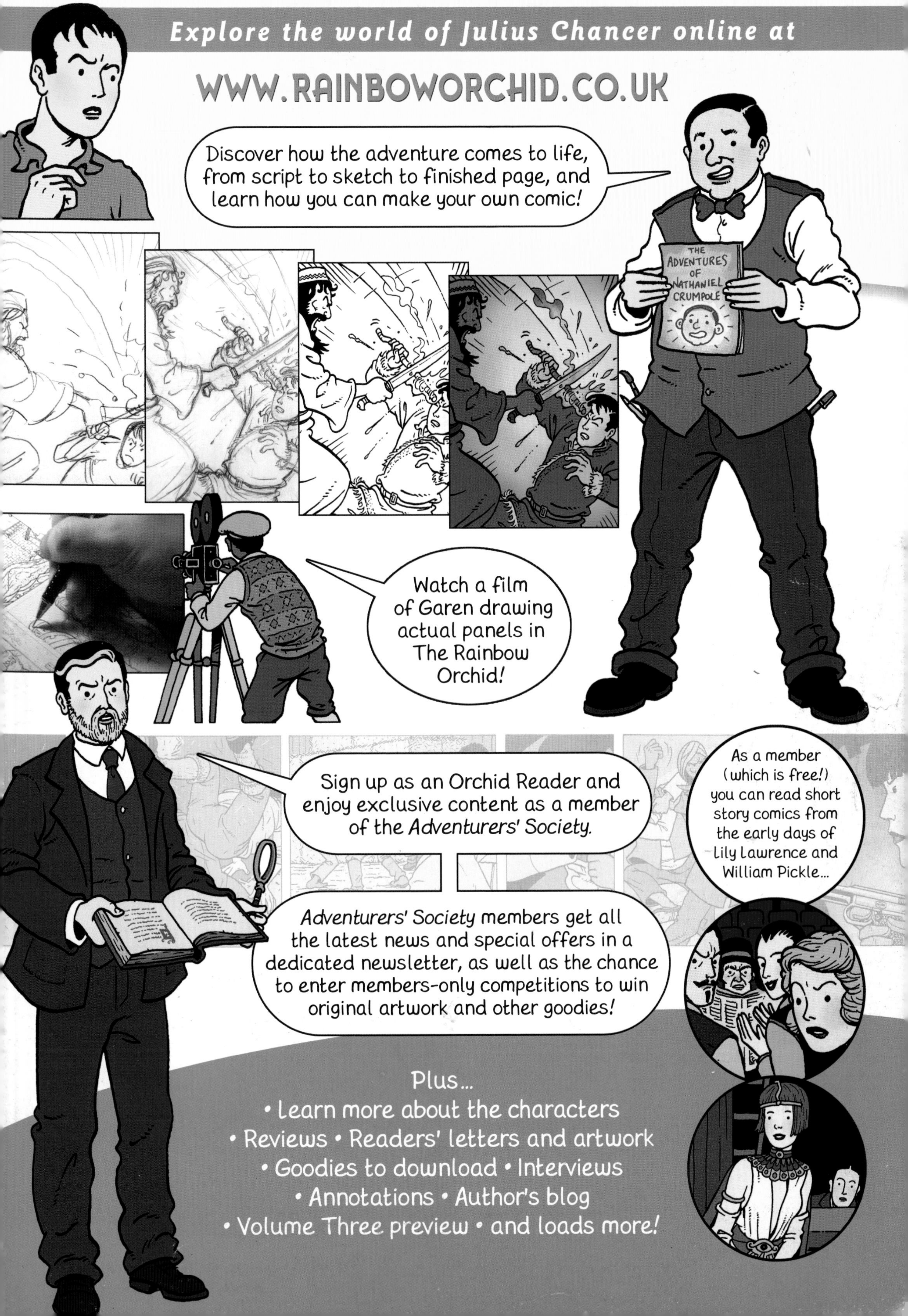

Explore the world of Julius Chancer online at
WWW.RAINBOWORCHID.CO.UK
Discover how the adventure comes to life, from script to sketch to finished page, and learn how you can make your own comic!
THE ADVENTURES OF NATHANIEL CRUMPOLE
Watch a film of Garen drawing actual panels in The Rainbow Orchid!
Sign up as an Orchid Reader and enjoy exclusive content as a member of the *Adventurers' Society*.
As a member (which is free!) you can read short story comics from the early days of Lily Lawrence and William Pickle...
Adventurers' Society members get all the latest news and special offers in a dedicated newsletter, as well as the chance to enter members-only competitions to win original artwork and other goodies!
Plus...
• Learn more about the characters
• Reviews • Readers' letters and artwork
• Goodies to download • Interviews
• Annotations • Author's blog
• Volume Three preview • and loads more!

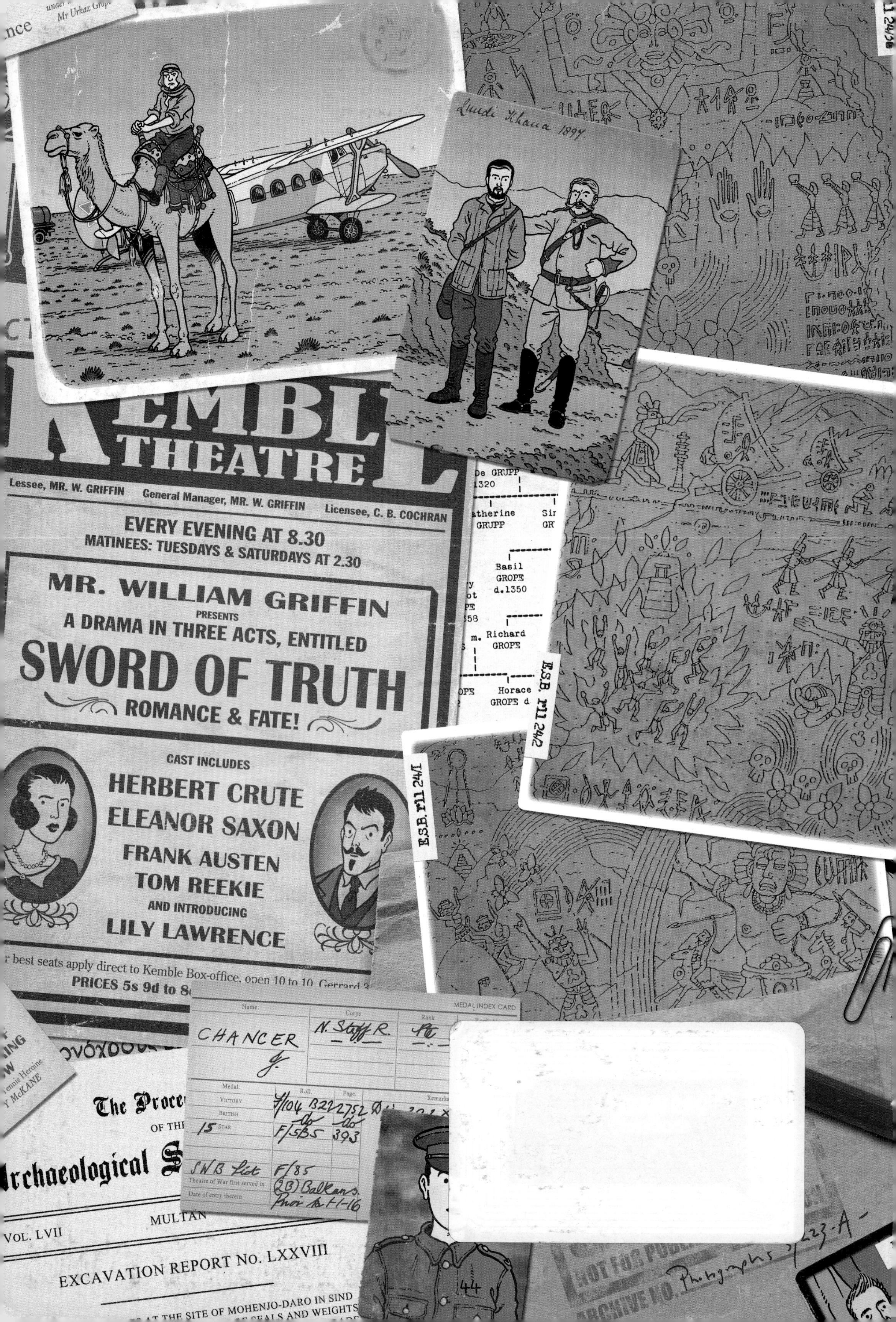
Mr Urkaz Grope
Lundi Khana 1894
KEMBLE
THEATRE
Lessee, MR. W. GRIFFIN
General Manager, MR. W. GRIFFIN
Licensee, C. B. COCHRAN
EVERY EVENING AT 8.30
MATINEES: TUESDAYS & SATURDAYS AT 2.30
MR. WILLIAM GRIFFIN
PRESENTS
A DRAMA IN THREE ACTS, ENTITLED
SWORD OF TRUTH
ROMANCE & FATE!
CAST INCLUDES
HERBERT CRUTE
ELEANOR SAXON
FRANK AUSTEN
TOM REEKIE
AND INTRODUCING
LILY LAWRENCE
r best seats apply direct to Kemble Box-office, open 10 to 10. Gerrard 3
PRICES 5s 9d to 8
De GRUPP
1320
atherine
GRUPP
Basil
GROPE
d.1350
m. Richard
GROPE
Horace
GROPE d
E.S.B. f11 24/2
E.S.B. f11 24/1
MEDAL INDEX CARD
Name
Corps
Rank
CHANCER
J.
N. Staff R.
Medal.
Roll.
Page.
Remarks
VICTORY
BRITISH
15 STAR
F/104 B22
2752
do
do
F/5B5
393
SWB List
F/85
Theatre of War first served in
(2B) Balkans.
Date of entry therein
Prior to 1-1-16
Tennis Heroine
Y McKANE
The Proce
OF THE
Archaeological S
MULTAN
VOL. LVII
EXCAVATION REPORT No. LXXVIII
AT THE SITE OF MOHENJO-DARO IN SIND
OF SEALS AND WEIGHTS
44
NOT FOR PUBLI
ARCHIVE NO. Photographs 5/223-A-